little Miss Magic

by Roger Hargreaves

Early one Monday morning in summer, Little Miss Magic awoke in the bedroom of Abracadabra Cottage.

Which was where she lived.

She yawned a yawn.

And got out of bed.

She went to the bathroom to clean her teeth.

"Squeeze," she said to the tube of toothpaste.

And, guess what?

The tube of toothpaste jumped up, and squeezed itself onto Little Miss Magic's toothbrush.

Honestly!

Little Miss Magic isn't called Little Miss Magic for nothing.

When she tells something to do something, it does it!

She went downstairs to the kitchen.

"Boil," she said to the kettle.

And it did!

"Toast," she said to the toaster.

"Spread," she said to a knife.

And the knife jumped up and spread some butter onto the toast.

"Pour," she said to the coffee pot.

And she sat down to breakfast.

Don't you wish you could make things do things like that?

She was enjoying a second cup of coffee when there was a knock at the kitchen door.

"Open," she said to the door.

And, as it did, there stood Mr Happy, looking exactly the opposite.

"You don't look your usual self," remarked Little Miss Magic. "What's the matter?"

"Everything," replied Mr Happy.

"Come in and tell me about it," she said.

"Have a cup of coffee."

"Pour," she said to the coffee pot.

"Now," said Little Miss Magic. "What is it?"

"It's Mr Tickle," replied Mr Happy. "He's become absolutely impossible!"

"What do you mean?" asked Little Miss Magic.

"Well," went on Mr Happy. "He used to go around tickling people every now and then, but now he's going around tickling people all the time!"
He sighed.

Little Miss Magic looked at him.

"It can't be that bad," she said.

"It's worse," said Mr Happy, unhappily.

"Cheer up," she grinned.

"Come on," she said.

And off they set from Abracadabra Cottage.

"After you," said Little Miss Magic to Mr Happy.

"Close," she said to the door.

Mr Tickle was in full cry!

What a Monday morning he was having!

He'd tickled Mr Mean until he'd moaned!

And Mr Greedy until he'd groaned!

And Little Miss Sunshine until she'd shivered!

And Mr Quiet until he'd quivered!

And Little Miss Plump until she'd pleaded!

And Little Miss Shy until she'd sobbed!

Not to mention the postman, a policeman, the doctor, three dogs, two cats!

And a worm!

"Aha," cried Mr Tickle as he spied Little Miss Magic and Mr Happy.

"Anyone for TICKLES?"

And he rushed up to them, reaching out those extraordinarily long arms of his, with those particularly ticklish fingers on the ends of them.

Little Miss Magic looked at Mr Happy.

"I see what you mean," she said.

And winked.

She pointed at Mr Tickle's extraordinarily long right arm.

"Shrink," she said.

And then she pointed to Mr Tickle's extraordinarily long left arm.

"Shrink," she said again.

And, as you remember, when Little Miss Magic tells something to do something, it does it!

Mr Tickle's arms were suddenly not extraordinarily long.

They were extraordinarily ordinary!

"That's not FAIR!" he cried. "You've spoiled my FUN!"

"It might have been fun for you," remarked Mr Happy. "But it wasn't much fun for anybody else."

"Come and see me tomorrow," said Little Miss Magic to Mr Tickle.

"There," she said to Mr Happy. "Happy now?"

Mr Happy smiled that famous smile of his.

"I'll say," he said.

"Come on," he added. "I'll buy you lunch."

And off they went to his favourite restaurant.

Smilers!

On Tuesday Mr Tickle went round to Abracadabra Cottage.

He knocked at the front door.

"Open," said a voice inside.

"Oh hello," smiled Little Miss Magic as the door opened by itself and she saw who was standing there.

"Come in!"

"I expect you'd like me to make your arms long again?" she said.

"Oh yes please," said Mr Tickle.

"Very well," she said.

Mr Tickle's face lit up.

"On one condition," she added.

His face fell.

"You are only allowed one tickle a day!"

"ONE tickle a DAY?" said Mr Tickle.

"That's not much!"

"Promise," said Little Miss Magic.

Mr Tickle sighed.

"Promise," he said.

"Grow," said Little Miss Magic.

And both Mr Tickle's arms grew back to their original long length.

"Now don't forget," she reminded him. "One tickle a day!"

"Or else!" she added.

Mr Tickle went out through the door.

"Goodbye," she said to him.

"Shut," she said to the door.

Mr Tickle stood outside Little Miss Magic's cottage.

"Ah well," he thought. "One tickle a day is better than no tickles a day!"

It was then that he saw one of the downstairs windows of Abracadabra Cottage was open.

"One tickle a day," he thought.

And a small smile came to his face.

"One tickle a day," he thought.

And, on that Tuesday morning, as one of those extraordinarily long arms reached in through the open window of Abracadabra Cottage, the small smile on the face of Mr Tickle turned into a giant grin.

"One tickle a day," he thought.

Fantastic offers for Little Miss fans!

Collect all your Mr. Men or Little Miss books in these superb durable collectors' cases!
Only £5.99 inc. postage and packing, these wipe-clean, hard-wearing cases will give all your Mr. Men or Little Miss books a beautiful new home!

Keep track of your collection with this giant-sized double-sided Mr. Men and Little Miss Collectors' poster.
Collect 6 tokens and we will send you a brilliant giant-sized double-sided collectors' poster! Simply tape a £1 coin to cover postage and packaging in the space provided and fill out the form overleaf.

STICK £1 COIN HERE (for poster only)

Only need a few Little Miss or Mr. Men to complete your set? You can order any of the titles on the back of the books from our Mr. Men order line on 0870 787 1724. Orders should be delivered between 5 and 7 working days.

— TO BE COMPLETED BY AN ADULT —

To apply for any of these great offers, ask an adult to complete the details below and send this whole page with the appropriate payment and tokens, to: MR. MEN CLASSIC OFFER, PO BOX 715, HORSHAM RH12 5WG

☐ Please send me a giant-sized double-sided collectors' poster.

AND ☐ I enclose 6 tokens and have taped a £1 coin to the other side of this page.

☐ Please send me ☐ Mr. Men Library case(s) and/or ☐ Little Miss library case(s) at £5.99 each inc P&P

☐ I enclose a cheque/postal order payable to Egmont UK Limited for £...............

OR ☐ Please debit my MasterCard / Visa / Maestro / Delta account (delete as appropriate) for £...............

Card no. ☐☐☐☐☐☐☐☐☐☐☐☐☐☐☐☐☐☐☐   Security code ☐☐☐

Issue no. (if available) ☐   Start Date ☐☐/☐☐/☐☐   Expiry Date ☐☐/☐☐/☐☐

Fan's name: .... Date of birth: ....

Address: ....

....

.... Postcode: ....

Name of parent / guardian: ....

Email for parent / guardian: ....

Signature of parent / guardian: ....

Please allow 28 days for delivery. Offer is only available while stocks last. We reserve the right to change the terms of this offer at any time and we offer a 14 day money back guarantee. This does not affect your statutory rights. Offers apply to UK only.

☐ We may occasionally wish to send you information about other Egmont children's books. If you would rather we didn't, please tick this box.

Ref: LIM 001